Copyright © 2000 by Nord-Süd Verlag AG, Gossau Zürich, Switzerland
First published in Switzerland under the title *Ich bin MäuseKatzenBärenStark*.
English translation copyright © 2000 by North-South Books Inc.

First published in the United States, Great Britain, Canada,
Australia, and New Zealand in 2000 by North-South Books,
an imprint of Nord-Süd Verlag AG, Gossau Zürich, Switzerland.

Distributed in the United States by North-South Books Inc., New York.

Library of Congress Cataloging-in-Publication Data is available.
A CIP catalogue record for this book is available from The British Library.
ISBN 0-7358-1343-4 (trade binding) 10 9 8 7 6 5 4 3 2 1
ISBN 0-7358-1344-2 (library binding) 10 9 8 7 6 5 4 3 2 1
Printed in Belgium

For more information about our books, and the authors and artists
who create them, visit our web site: www.northsouth.com

Burny Bos

ALEXANDER THE GREAT

Illustrated by Hans de Beer

Translated by J. Alison James

North-South Books

New York · London

There was once a young mouse named Alexander, who dreamed of being big and brave like the comic book superhero, Mighty Bruno.

Alexander's mother worried that his dreams of glory would lead him into danger. "You must be careful, Alexander," she told him. "Mice should be cautious—not bold and daring."

In their home beneath the floor, the mouse family lived in safety. But up above, where the cat named Rats lived, it was terribly dangerous. Rats guarded the entrance to her domain like a tiger.

Once, Alexander had seen her left paw. One single paw, and it alone was twice his size—with big, sharp claws! Alexander was terrified of Rats.

All the mice were scared of Rats. But Alexander's father was the most afraid of all.

Whenever he heard the cat's name, a chill ran down his spine and his tail stump stood on end. Father Mouse had once had a long glorious tail, but Rats had bitten it off! Ever since that day, Father had not dared to venture above in search of food for the family.

One sunny day the mouse family sat at the table, hungrily waiting for their supper. But Mother Mouse came out of the kitchen with empty paws.

"We have nothing left to eat," she said quietly.

Father felt so guilty that he began to cry. Soon the whole family was crying because Father was crying. Only Alexander didn't cry. He squeezed his eyes tightly together so that no tears could slip out.

As Alexander lay in bed that night, he came up with a plan. He waited until the whole family was asleep. Then he slipped into his mother's room. He took out her fur coat and cut off a large piece. Then he spent the rest of the night sewing. By morning he had finished.

Alexander looked in the mirror. He tried standing on two legs. He felt strong and brave in his bear costume. How frightening I look! he thought proudly.

Alexander tiptoed past his sleeping family to the hole that led into the living room above. He mustered his great bear courage and poked his nose through the hole.

Rats was nowhere to be seen! Alexander breathed a sigh of relief. As fast as his little legs would carry him, he raced across the room to the kitchen. There, he stood up on two legs like a real bear and carefully peered inside. Still no Rats.

Alexander scurried up the sideboard and opened the door with his tiny paws. There lay a piece of cheese so large that Alexander couldn't even lift it! With all his strength, he shoved the cheese off the sideboard. It landed with a loud thump. Alexander froze. But there was still no sign of Rats.

Alexander climbed down the drawers to the floor and pushed the hunk of cheese inch by inch toward the hole. But when he finally got there, he found the hole was too small for the huge piece of cheese!

Alexander had to bite off smaller chunks of cheese and stuff them through the hole. He was so busy with his work that he didn't notice Rats looming behind him.

When the last bit of cheese had thumped to the floor below, Rats sunk her teeth into the back of Alexander's bear suit. Frozen with fright, Alexander dangled above those horrible, sharp claws. Oh, sweet Mother, he thought. I'll never see you again! Any second now, Rats will eat me. Alexander prepared himself for the worst, shivering with fright.

Rats carried Alexander to her basket and set him down among the kittens. Oh, heavens! There are more of them, thought Alexander. I'm to be a feast for them all!

Rats started licking Alexander's bear costume, purring noisily.

She must actually believe I'm one of her kittens! he thought, and the idea was so comforting, the round soft kittens so warm, and he himself so tired, that he fell fast asleep.

The next morning the mouse family found the chunks of cheese. Hungry as they all were, they stuffed themselves until their bellies were round and full.

Mother Mouse looked happily around at the group, only then noticing that Alexander was missing. Shocked, she jumped up and stumbled over his Mighty Bruno comic book. When she saw the snips of fur coat lying around, she remembered Alexander's dream and raced to the hole.

She looked about and, horrified, saw the huge head of Rats the cat. But then she saw three kittens and a cute little bear hopping along behind them all. She could breathe again. Her son was safe: Rats had adopted him.

Whenever the cat mother slept, Alexander brought delicious food from upstairs down to his family. Sometimes he stayed for a while and showed his brothers and sisters his comic books. But before Rats missed him, he had to be back upstairs, safely playing with his brother and sister cats. It was an adventurous life.

Alexander wasn't really fooling Rats. She knew he was bringing his mouse family food, and let him get away with it. Even after the other kittens had grown ten times as big as him, she still didn't eat Alexander. She knew very well that he was a mouse, but she had come to love him.

And Alexander loved his new life. He felt strong and brave even though his bear suit was worn-out, and he was content to slip back and forth between his two loving families.